# HIGGLEDY PIGGLEDY
# HOBBLEDY HOY

# HIGGLEDY PIGGLEDY HOBBLEDY HOY

By Dorothy Butler

Illustrated by Lyn Kriegler

GREENWILLOW BOOKS

NEW YORK

Watercolor paints, colored pencils, and pen and colored inks were used
for the full-color art.    The text type is ITC Esprit Medium.
Text copyright © 1991 by Dorothy Butler
Illustrations copyright © 1991 by Lyn Kriegler
First Edition
10  9  8  7  6  5  4  3  2  1

Library of Congress Cataloging-in-Publication Data
Butler, Dorothy (date)
Higgledy piggledy hobbledy hoy / by Dorothy Butler;
pictures by Lyn Kriegler.
p.  cm.
Summary: On the way to a picnic, a little girl and a
little boy make up nasty rhymes about each other.
ISBN 0-688-08660-8.   ISBN 0-688-08661-6 (lib. bdg.)
[1. Picnicking—Fiction.   2. Stories in rhyme.]
I. Kriegler, Lyn, ill.   II. Title.
PZ8.3.B9775Hi   1991   [E]—dc20
89-77503   CIP   AC

For Simon and Susan,
the original
good little, bad little
boy and girl
— D. B.


For Tom
— L. K.

Higgledy piggledy hobbledy hoy,

A good little girl and a bad little boy.

Jiggery pokery rackety poo,

It's good little me and it's bad little you.

Fiddledy diddledy twiddle and twirl,

A slow little boy and a fast little girl.

Wiffley waffley widdledy wee,

It's slow little you and it's fast little me.

Higgledy piggledy hobbledy hoy,

A bad little girl and a good little boy.

Jiggery pokery rackety poo,

It's good little me and it's bad little you.

Fiddledy diddledy twiddle and twirl,

A fast little boy and a slow little girl.

Wiffley waffley widdledy wee,

It's slow little you and it's fast little me.

Abracadabra! Bring on the lunch!

Cheesecake, cherry pie, munch, munch, munch!

Ice cream, watermelon, lemonade plus—

For good little, fast little, wonderful US!

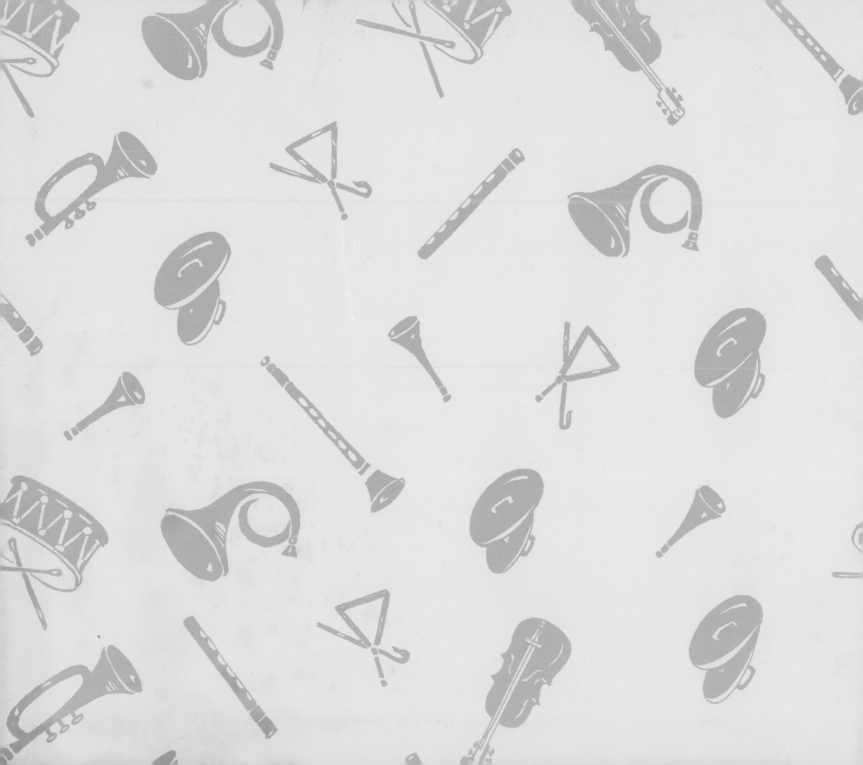